YIKES!

It's Scary Story Time

To Emmerich and Elodie,
Happy Spoo-oo-oo-ky reading!

Jon Stahl

by Jon Stahl
Art by Charles McNall

For my students, past and present,
at P.S. 84 and Stephen S. Wise.
May you enjoy reading this as much as
I've enjoyed reading to all of you.

CONTENTS

FOREWORD

I loved hearing ghost stories as a kid at camp. I would roast marshmallows by a campfire, a little spooked out, but still savor every word I heard.

Some stories in this book are funny. Some are spooky. Some may even give you a shiver. And that's all right! Feeling a bit scared and overcoming that feeling is an important part of growing up.

So curl up by the nearest campfire, break out the marshmallows, and get ready to have some spooky fun!

THE VIPER

A man and his wife were cleaning their house when the phone rang.

"Hello?" said the man.

A voice on the other end said, "I am the Viper. I am six blocks away..."

The man hung up the phone. "Uh oh" he said.

The phone rang again. The woman picked it up. "Hello?" she said.

"I am the Viper. I am four blocks away..."

"Uh oh" said the woman. The phone rang again. This time they both picked it up.

"I am the Viper. I am two
blocks away..."
"Uh oh," they said together.
They hung up the phone.
Then they waited. And waited.
And waited...
A knock came at their door.

They looked at the door.

They looked at each other.

"Uh oh" they said.

They walked to the door.

They opened it.

They gasped!

Standing there was a little man with a bucket and a sponge.

With an accent he said "I am the Viper. I came to vipe the vindows!"

O' HAPPY MONSTERS

Have you ever seen a skeleton
Surfing on the waves?

Have you ever seen a zombie

Sweeping up the graves?

Have you ever seen a boogeyman
Dancing on a train?

Have you ever seen a swamp thing,
Swimming in the rain?

Have you ever seen a wolfman
Howling at the sun?
Have you ever seen a group of
monsters
Having so much fun!

THE BOY WHO DIDN'T KNOW

Once there was a boy named Haley. He was like all the other boys in almost every way. He liked to play sports. He liked to laugh at jokes. He liked to make messes. One day a boy in Haley's class named Peter invited all the boys to his birthday party.

Except for Haley.

Haley was sad. Why wasn't he invited too? He liked to play sports. He liked to laugh at jokes.

He liked to make messes!
Haley ran to the bathroom and
cried. He didn't understand it. Why
wasn't he invited to the party?

Just then the bathroom door opened and Peter and another boy came in. Haley hid in the corner. He listened to what the boys were saying. "I wish Haley could be at my party," Peter said sadly. "Me too," said the other boy. "I miss him."

"Yeah," said Peter. They left. Haley came out of the corner. He didn't get what the boys meant. He looked in the mirror. And then he knew what they meant.

Haley had no reflection.

He was a ghost!

THE REFRIGERATOR

One day a girl named Sidney was babysitting some kids. They had lots of fun. They watched a movie on TV. They made a castle out of couch pillows. They popped popcorn on the stove. At eight O'clock Sidney put the kids to bed. "Good night, you two," she said and turned off the light.

Sidney was watching TV, when the phone rang.

"Hello?" she answered.

A spooky voice said, "Check the refrigerator…"

Sidney went into the kitchen. She opened the fridge. She looked inside. Everything looked normal. She went back to watching TV. The phone rang. "Check the refrigerator…" said the same spooky voice.

Sidney went into the kitchen
again. She opened the refrigerator.
Everything looked fine.

She went back to watch TV.
The phone rang yet again.
She answered it.
"Check the refrigerator..." said the
spooky voice.
Sidney was getting fed up with this.

But she went anyway. She slowly opened the refrigerator door…she looked inside. She screamed!

A salad was scattered about! Carrots and lettuce and cucumbers everywhere!

It was a big, big mess.

The phone rang in her hand.
Sidney jumped! She answered it. It
was the police.

"We've tracked the call! It's coming
from inside the house!"

Sidney turned
around. She screamed
again.

Standing in the
doorway...was an
evil tomato with a cell
phone!

DON'T BE LATE

I came to class late one day.
"Jonah, you're late. You need to stay
in for recess," my teacher said. "Oh
man..." I said.
After lunch, all the other kids went
out to play. I went back to my
classroom. I was late.
Again.
"Jonah, you're late," said my
teacher. "I'm sorry" I said. "Don't
be late again," he said.

I cleaned the erasers. I put the library books in order. I did a worksheet. It was no fun.

My teacher said, "Okay, Jonah, you can go out to recess now. But don't be late again..."

The next day, I was late.

Again.

"No recess today, Jonah." My teacher said. "Oh man..." I said.

After lunch, all the other kids went out to play. I went back to my classroom. I was late.

Again.

I went inside my class. I knew my teacher would not be happy.

But he wasn't there.

"Hello...?" I called. There was no answer. I sat and waited. Then a voice came from behind me.

"I told you not to be late." I turned around.

It was my teacher. But he wasn't just my teacher. He was a vampire!

A real Vampire!

I ran out of the room.

And from that day on, I was never late again.

MONSTER EXPERT

Ghosts are never funny,

Ghouls are always mean.

Dracula's never sunny,

Frankenstein's always green.

The Mummy's never naked,

A werewolf wears no clothes.
I'd tell you more 'bout monsters,
But this is all I knows!

THE BOX

One day, Max walked by a store with lots of things in the window. There were strange masks and weird outfits and odd toys. Max was curious, so he went inside.

The owner of the store smiled at Max. "Welcome to my store!" he said. "You can buy anything you wish. Except for that box over there." Max looked at the box. It was black and creepy looking.

"What's in that box?" Max asked.

"Pay it no mind," said the owner.

"Buy something else." But Max was curious. He wanted to know what was in the box. A noise came from the box. It was like a low growl. "Is an animal in there?" Max asked. "Pay it no mind," said the owner. "I can sell you a nice mask." Max didn't want a mask. He wanted to know what was in the box.

The owner went into the back to look for something. Max went closer to the box. The box moved a little. Max went even closer. The box shook. Max went closer. The box made a scratchy noise. Max reached out a hand.

Max started to open the lid...

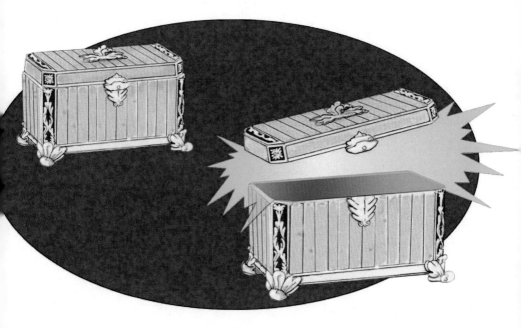

The box screamed!

Max ran out of the store. He ran far away.

He never found out what was in the box.

THE GIRL ON THE BEACH

It was a hot day at the beach. Tyra sat near her parents, building a sand castle. A girl in a red and white bathing suit came up to her. "Can I help?" the girl asked. "Okay," said Tyra. They built the castle tall and wide.

"That looks great!" said Tyra. "Do you want to go for a swim?" The girl in the red and white bathing suit looked at the water. She shook her head. "I can't swim," she said. She looked sad.

"Oh." Tyra felt bad for her. "Do you want to build another sand castle then?" she asked. "No," said the girl. She looked out at the water. "I have to go now. They're calling me." "Who is?" Tyra asked. She turned to look at the sea. There was no one there. She turned back, but the girl was gone.

Tyra went back to her family. Her dad was reading the newspaper. "This is so sad," said Tyra's dad. "What is?" asked Tyra's mom. "This story in the newspaper," said Tyra's dad. "A girl drowned yesterday." Tyra asked, "Was she wearing a red and white bathing suit?"

Her dad put down the newspaper. "How did you know?" he asked. Tyra didn't answer. She just looked at the water.

Where the stories come from

"The Viper" is a story I first heard at camp in 1986, but I'm sure it's been around a lot longer than that. I remember being so relieved when the ending turned out to be funny!

"O Happy Monsters" and *"Monster Expert"* are original poems of mine.

"The Boy Who Didn't Know" and *"The Girl on the Beach"* are original stories I came up with, but both owe a great deal to movies where characters don't know until the end of the story that they're ghosts.

"The Refrigerator" is based on an urban legend that I heard as a kid, also at camp. I decided to make it silly instead of scary at the end.

"Don't Be Late" and *"The Box"* are original stories of mine.

I hope you enjoyed reading *Yikes! It's Scary Story Time* as much as I enjoyed writing it!

Jon Stahl, Studio City CA

October 2013

Bio

Jon Stahl is a teacher, a writer, and a filmmaker.

He lives with his wife Wendy,

and their two guinea pigs,

Hubert and Peanut.

Made in United States
North Haven, CT
12 October 2021

10299666R00031